The Paladin Guardian volume I

The Hellenic Princess

Raina Shiba

ISBN 978-93-5610-440-2
© Raina Shiba 2022
Published in India 2022 by Pencil

A brand of

One Point Six Technologies Pvt. Ltd.
123, Building J2, Shram Seva Premises,
Wadala Truck Terminal, Wadala (E)
Mumbai 400037, Maharashtra, INDIA
E connect@thepencilapp.com
W www.thepencilapp.com

Author biography

This book is an attempt to claim that 'Nothing is Impossible' if one has the inertia and the determination to fight against the current. There are no setbacks or inhibitions as it is just the creation of our mind and ourselves construct it around us. We tend to go by the convictions of the world and judge ourselves on their impressions, instead, do what makes one happy and content and let the rest will follow.

I am just a simpleton with dreams. I have lived in Mumbai India throughout my life. I have two children, and a set of students who are very close to my heart and have always encouraged me in my writing.

CONTENTS

Chapter 1-Corinth

Dawn and the pale fresh rays of the sun blanketed the city of Calloth with a revelation of hope; a recognition of existence. The trust and confidence unfurled as the city brightened up every moment with the scintillating sun that conveyed; the darkness has gone, gather yourselves, the role is set for yet another day.

The day was no different for the 'Calloth Mansion'. The night faded away and the glistening sun promulgated, the mist swaddled magnificence of the mansion with a backdrop of the serrated mountains looming in the distance, the heaven-touching apex of the mountain drenched in heavenly light, the thick green hills glinted screening a picturesque view of the mansion. The flowers that bloomed in the vicinity emitted a honey-sweet smell adding to the subtle aura and a gentle warmth cloaked the place. The mansion was a unique antique structure, as I would say, like the 11th-century Greco-Roman classical structure of 'The Manor House'. A moated castle with a grand entrance and a drawbridge; lay dropped and dilapidated, its functionaries obsolete and a grand gate in lineage with the high wall. To the left of the gate is a sloppy metal tent for the watch, and there he was 'the watcher' so to say but had a better role to play Mr Warbhinger, who sleeps day and night with his eyes open, probably polished it over the years as a defence mechanism.

Mr Warbhinger a tall, gaunt figure with a mysterious questionable expression; could get one peek into the soul, always in his uniform and on duty, I guess!

The mansion looked like a major element of domestique architecture with a huge garden, and exorbitant front views mainly of stone and wood. A well-planned architecture with a tall front and two adjacent buildings clustered to perform the frontage with semi-tall structures and less evident floors behind; presumably to a count of four or five. The wall with a flat surface at the centre of the structure rose to a sculpted coat of arms and an empty flag post above it. A small landscaped garden less cared for, shrubs growing throughout the lawn and structured plant growth flanking the pathway to the entrance, with brick and stone layered out to the entrance of the building. A grand marble fountain with intricately carved structures of damsels; that looked like the tree nymphs around the urn, standing out above the piles of cascaded rocks upon which the raining water fell, dry moss in the basin and dry algae on its rocky cascade, apparently yearning to quench. The damsels had beautiful features though parts of the sculpture had worn out and the ornamental beauty and complexion had faded, yet they looked strikingly real. Tall trees captured the view around the house spread over an unmoved lawn that ran around with dehydrated grass that could catch fire if the sun glows too hard and shrubs of petit flowers around, many wild and some sprung from the pollen buried from flower plants-history today.

The house, one of the hostels of 'The Calloth University' gleaming like a silver-gold tray with its fluorescent yellow exterior and the glowing white interior section, looked promising each day.

Just before noon; 1st May 3029, the exorbitant long steps at the entrance suddenly got busy, the steps flocked like a swarm of bees, by the inhabitants of the hostel. The hustle-bustle and intermittent frolicking permeated the air- the result of the notice displayed in the foyer of The Caloth University

It read:

'The college hereby notify, the commencement of the 3rd trimester 3028-3029 scheduled in May. It is also notified that there will be no further intimation regarding the same, the syllabus is as mentioned by your respective department heads and the date sheet will follow soon.

Mr Shiroesqui.

Mr shiroesqui, fondly called Hiro by the students, is the only resort in the university for any assistance due to his proximity to the admin. He was the director's assistant and handled all the matters associated with the boarding house.

Gradually, the steps of the house began to enfold with a counterpane of books, papers and above all clusters of students. Jabbering and mumbling echoed;" let me see the 'portending danger' notes" "Can someone help me with the 'cosmic portions' notes. There were students of every level preparing for the upcoming exam, when a soft but bold voice was heard hastily coming out of the hostel, "Could anyone share with me the notes on colours anecdotes". Instantly numerous hands were stretching out the notes with jinks outroar, "Here...".

It was Himu the heartthrob for many considered by his hostel mates as a role model. A fair-complexioned boy of medium height. He had an obedient disposition, with a smile well enough to grab attention and the charm to take people into his confidence. Himu is a very popular member of the university, popular has much to say, with many fan followers for his style and wits.

Himu was normally the first choice for all the girls and then it was Garvithino and they called him Thino, who was Himu's friend but had an inclination towards Nish for reasons unknown. Prathamiso fondly called Miso a cause of his gentle nature, a normal statured boy slim, very understanding and would easily have a 'Yes' to his tone. He has a sharp inclination towards Nish-Nishthani. Nisthani is a beautiful, tall girl with lovely lustrous hair and loved writing poetries. Her college mates call Nish and there is a lot about Nish, which would gradually unfold.

'Do any of you have 'The manifestation symbols book?' asked a gentle sound.

'Yes, Miso, I have it, I do not need it now" replied Miach "But, when will you return it?"

'You give now! I will return it as soon as possible' Miso affirmed.

Silence reigned with intermittent flipping of the pages or by the rifling of loose paper with the wind. The soft chirping of the swallows melodiously permeated amidst total ignorance. The wind flipped and flapped the un-swept leaves on the tiled path, which rose at the gush of air and danced down to touch the floor like a child enthralled while swinging. There was intermittent rumbling when the dry leaves swept berserk with the flow of the wind.

She stepped through the drawbridge and into the huge delimbed iron gate. A coil of rattling passed through the tall trees like a hoot of dismay and leaves substantiating the blustering wind. She walked through the squiggly pathway; The silence disrupted by the crisp twigs crunching under her feet and the rumbling of her suitcase. She walked steadily with an aura around her. She could sense the movements around her and her smile acknowledged them. The forsaken shrubs of the flowering chrysanthemums, which lay unattended for seasons no count, began to bloom and emitted a sweet aroma to fill the place. The grass in the lawn area began swaying with the breeze that wafted and an enchantment filled the air, as she passed through the pathway. She examined the place around and arrived in front of the flocked students, who were least aware of what was happening.

She stood there basking in the little patches of sunshine that dappled her face, she scoffed to catch some attention, but in vain. Attempted it again, without any response. Timidly and daintily, she said, 'I am Giselle, and I would like to know,' after a pause she continues, 'Where is my room is-131? can someone help me?'.

There was no response, she repeated it, and the silence continued! She gathered herself together and scornfully retorted,' Can you please give me the way, I have to get to room 131'. She gasped.

A wave of astonishment triggered the minuscule crowd and caught their attention, as they looked up at her agape, just to witness a meekly naïve girl with profound beauty and a slim figure standing, her eyes were Mediterranean Blue. There was no sign of any apoplectic rage in her and stood calmly awaiting a reply. She was dressed, well! With a long gown custom made to fit her convenience, an aquamarine locket significantly showed on her neck and her golden hair glowed in competition with the rays of the sun, with stiff strands flying across her face tracing the wind. She stood there intimidated and calm with her rolling bag, a cage and an umbrella standing tall to reach her arms with lacey frills.

Instantly, Himu, the gentle boy stood up to greet her, 'Hi, I am Himashinnus, they call me 'Himu'. 'Room 131 is on the 3rd floor and we are all………' he paused…

And another got up from in between the group and dusting her dress from behind said" Yes, Heman! Extending her hand to shake "Hi! I am Miach, as they call me" "welcome to our university".

Giselle was passive and did not heed their approach to friendship. She showed no signs of attention; instead, she again asked," Can you show me my room? Her pretentious innocence spilt all over her face, while her eyes scanned the place like searchlights and were as distractive as a toddling. Probably, she was looking for something, when unanticipatedly the blustering wind rattled the leaves, she drew her attention to the tree close by.

Now, the tree; which stood like an umbrella short and stout, with its branches and thick juicy leaves scanning the sky and white flowers with a slight pinkish tinge on its waxy petals gazing down.

Flowers, not a common glance, with a twisted bulb from its core as though it has conceived fluid and succulent with juicy uneven gross petals, normally seen with drippings. They were called the Stephanotis Debbie, with no appreciable factor of beauty but having a strong fragrance very difficult to judge appreciable or not, this enveloped 2 meters circumference around the plant. The leaves were sharp-edged with a pointed tip and were compound. The branches had some thin tentacles dropping down and a malnourished trunk; swayed nonchalantly, whispering as Giselle approached the tree. The whispering Truly, the tree had all the reason to be evaded off by the inhabitants of the hostel as it gave a strange feeling near it and the flower was not appeasing at all. Giselle slowly drifted walked towards the tree, as she closed to its proximity her face brightened up and close buds bloomed, she gleefully stretched her hands and plucked a flower, she began admiring its beauty. The effusing fragrance captured her delight and a grin; ear to ear flashed…

The onlookers at the hostel thought amazed, 'Weird, isn't it!!! The children looked on astounded again and Himu stood dazed, with the incomplete conversation…….

Chapter 2-The Incantators

The Sun, almost overhead, as the warmth began spreading its coverall, pangs of hunger struck hard… Gradually, the students sitting at a distance began to dissipate into the hostel. Few rushed down the steps, grabbed their cycles kept grooved into its slots near the entrance and began to disperse. They lived scattered in the city or its suburbs. They bid their friends, slowly lifting into the thin air as the propellers swished swashed; whipping the air they ceased leaving a visible trail behind.

Himu, yet dazed by what had happened, stood still as his mind racked, 'This hasn't happened… ever! unbelievable uhh!' 'How could such a thing happen' he thought.

As Giselle returned to the steps, where the others were awaiting her still dazed. Miach picks up from where Himu stops; '0Hi, Giselle!' 'Glad to meet you. She starts talking to her to know more…

Miach and Himu were arch-enemies, though they grew up together as their parents were good acquaintances, Popular families hailing from the same city 'Migniana'. Now, Migniana, is one of the flourishing cities of the country 'Milletus, The kingdom of Shinisus'. The eclectically designed city is magnificently placed amidst Greco-Roman architecture as the city has a history of its own. Flowers stay bloomed; bloomed of various sizes and shapes, capable of emitting a plurality of discrete scents, which permeated the environment containing the disposition of the forms of good. Though they disposed of the good but can at times be lethal, rightly; It can flood and choke you. Trees, lush-green and tall, stood like watchtowers, as guards to the city.

An extension of the Corinth Greek empire has a saga of itself and is safeguarded by great warriors.

 Himu's father, Sir Megnanissus a man of great valour. He was a fighter with the single string wave power; 'The concatenate-demrrihe' could seize and tumble a pillar, or uproot a bunch of high-rise oak trees with a single string pull.

Miach's father, Sir Prakinasus was also in the army with his powerful techno-wave. This was very dangerous and could pierce through, and distort or destroy the internal organs of living things, but there was a catch in his ability, his mind could sense and map the waves to destruction. The waves were fatal and yes, they can devastate from the inside like a tsunami. Sir Prakinasus also could sense any offensive wave that could come his way with the power to devour a whole army at a time. These two powerful men are known as veteran wizards in the court of His Majesty Puissant-Shinisus son of the great wizard his highness Majodar-shinisus from the Shinisus dynasty. They ruled the planet and safeguarded the planet from wizards of other galaxies, as they claim existence. Himu and Miach are well equipped with the innate qualities of ostentatious splendour. Ohh! I missed it, this makes them popular and gregarious amongst their college mates.

Back in the hostel, Miach leaves no stone unturned against Himu, "Hey, Himu, you got dissed".

"La La La, there is someone now, who is with me" she tattles sarcastically and she gradually draws closer to Giselle and continues, "I hope she just does not…" and pushes up her nose with her thumb to tease Himu.

"Hey Giselle, I am Mahekmathini, those boisterous call me Miach. I am your roomy, was expecting one". She said, 'Weirdo' thought she.

Giselle stood in silence trying to contain her suitcase and a cage sort box, least bothered to reply and distressed to go to her room.

Miach looking at the cage, 'Hey, what's in it? A pet!" she exclaims. Giselle stays silent, Miach peeks into the cage, and continues," It is a cute little tiny badger, what is its name? and why do you have a badger as your pet, weirdo? She says and taps her as is how she's to her friends…

Gizelle does not reply, shakes hands and slowly walks with Miach towards the hostel. Himu is still bedazzled and glued to the steps as the girls approached them, he heads them off, disappointed and settles on the beading of the steps. Kanov quickly followed him and exclaimed, 'Hey buddy, she is new, why sore your heart, let it be'. Kanov is a very composed and soft-spoken girl with her mesmerizing ability in chemicals and talent to convince. Miach and Giselle close in and the other members of the group also edge in…

"Hi, I am Garvithinous, alias Thino and he is Miso our nerd," said Garvithinous as he tagged into the group with Miso.

Miach "yeah, call him Lac" this took Gizelle by surprise, but she calmly listened to their conversation and exclaimed, "lac!?"

Miach starts grabbing Thino's hands. Thino strive's to resist Miach but he fails her preponderance built and she pulls his t-shirt to expose a part of his belly; as fair as paper, as white as milk. Thino flinched, murmuring trying to push her away but then…

"Look at him, he is white as milk, so I call him lac; milk", Himu contradicts, "And look at her, Macho man" and tries to support Thino, he continues, "Beware, she can trip you down or even carry you, true macho!" which follows with a low-voiced wrangle that sets in amongst them. Himu always had a contradictory remark for Micah and an undercurrent of antipathy amongst them, though Miach was always positive and cared two hooks for any such remarks.

On watcher, Giselle amused, curbs her expression and suppresses her conception. She thinks, 'There's time…How foolish…They are interesting!'.

The group again begins to stir and chatter about their exam preparation ignoring Giselle's presence as the heat was on.

Giselle out of notice, slowly wends up towards the entry door, trying to pull her suitcase up, with the little case suspended on her baggage.

The box lost its control in her hands and it vigorously lurched from one side to the other, followed by a frantic twitting. The pet case was also pendulating with the valise and the mild trilling sound could be heard. Her long skirt was trapped at her feet, her shoes clasped onto the stairs at their heels making it difficult to scale the stairs and to add to the trauma, her hat also dropped from her head. She looked at the hat and it returned to its original position and remained there but huffed and stooped down laboriously to untangle the matted fabric.

Undeterred, she began ascending, her muscle pulling sending electrifying impulse of pain, as she was lean with a timid constitution. Suddenly, she and her baggage fell into a rhythmic climb as though it was commanded to convey her to the veranda; her bags seemed to share a lift too, still unnoticed by the group. A sudden gush of wind; restless as an infant and gathering the leaves around into its whirl, blew her hat away and unclipped her hair lock to unfold her beautiful straight long hair, with a golden glace as the sunlight fell on it. Giselle looked back and smiled as she saw the illusioned nymph figure with her hand upright commanding nature.

On arrival at the huge, sort of veranda, she daunted seeing a lady, tall, medium healthy; wearing some kind of a uniform with some star badges on her, standing in front of the door. She had a shrewd expression, with a little masculinity for her features with a broad chin and little over thick brows. The fair-complexioned lady stood with her hands crossed against her chest and not the slightest sign of pleasance. She looked at Giselle, who stood with her feet glued, eager about the next outcome.

The unpleasant look caused a threat of danger, Giselle took a few steps ahead and said, "I am Giselle, I am new here and I wanted……." before she could complete, a shrill crept through her spine, when a coarse roar fired with a blast from the lady's canon mouth,

"Himanshinno, Mahekmanthini…"

At that call, the children sprang into action and a sudden thumping of footsteps resounded as the group ran up to the lady.

'Yes ma'am, yes ma'am, yes ma'am, echoed, followed by a ……

Chapter 3-The magnificence

The children ran towards the lady and gathered around her 'Yes ma'am', prompted Thino. She looked at him and furiously said," Why are you not aiding her"? Gently turned to Giselle, 'Good afternoon child, is it long you arrived?' she addressed Giselle with a succumbed voice,' You are welcome'.   Giselle nodded submissively.

MIach," Let me introduce her, she is Madame Nagasevani, the matron and caretaker of this hostel and her abilities" she stops and continues," Hmmm, you will know in time'.

Madam Nagaseveni looked at Thino again and sounded tigerish, 'Yes, what is so pleasant about your, 'Yes, ma'am? she continued, 'Do you have any understanding about how you deal with a new student'. She continued fuming 'Is it right to be engrossed in yourselves and not attending to the new hostel member, aren't you supposed to help her out". She sounded harsh and belligerent.

A tide of chattering rippled, 'What; who is she?', 'What is so important about her?', 'Why so much importance?. 'Hush, quiet all', retorted Madame Nagasevani, "Just do as I say, Miach take her to the room, she is your roomy', then looking at the others 'Rest of you make haste for lunch, or I will shut down the dining room', at this the students rushed into the entrance and gradually disappeared followed by the matron.

Mitch stayed back to escort Giselle into the hostel. Miach helped her with her luggage but her curious eyes were installed on the small cage box. As they entered Giselle was awe-struck at the resplendent splendorous hall with a very high dome ceiling and a huge chandelier that could be of at least a 4-5-metres radius with Bohemian crystals and fixtures of small metallic flowers. The walls were carved so well as though it real and living, the pillars supporting the ceiling sculpted beautifully with portraits of famous magicians, there was an array of flowers, buds and leaves on a white and pink background. It was contrary to the dull structure portrayed externally and was well illuminated with natural light from the transparent doom and tube natural light that crawled in from the walls, which also glistened crystals as light cast on it. The ambience was so beautiful that Giselle stood still looking at the ceiling.

Miach broke the spellbound silence, "Come, you have to register, I will show you. she took her to a sort of reception counter, where a man with a long beard. He was a man of very words or literally with no words, he suddenly sprung up on his feet as soon as they approached the counters and glanced at Giselle with a twinkle in his eye.

Miach, "Sir, she is Giselle, a new resident, she wants to register her name". The bearded man was Anisipsus and no one knew his age and when was he born and where he hails from. They say he is 2000 years old.

Anisipsus with a little jitter pulled out a huge register and began inscribing her name with a plume, yes, a magical plume; the plume just tapped at his fingers releasing itself and wrote

After completion, she stretched it before her and spoke with extreme humility, "Here ma'am, please sign". Giselle bowed to him graciously and completed the requirements.

Both the girls walked towards a wall painted with bright colours with Anisipsus eyes fixed on them, as they approached, the wall shattered into thin air and an impeccable spiral stair just pulled in front of them and spoke, "Where to? my dear madams". Miach signalled Giselle to embark on it, Miach boldly 'The third floor please'. The step jolted then flew with them, to be at their floor the next moment. They walked into the corridor followed by the rumble of her baggage, she glanced around to see the benignly fixed doors with torchlight intermittently placed in between the doors that buffed up the long-stretched pathway. Miach stopped at door 301 and plunged her hand into the left pocket and then the right looking, Giselle guessed,' Apparently looking for the key to the door, uh…, very absentminded'. The key could not be traced and sent her pondering to have Nish coming the next moment frantically to them and panting said, 'Miach, here's your key, you left it in the library this morning'.

Nish was Nishtani, also another member of the group. And Nish you are going. Miach, 'Giselle, this is Nish and Nish, this is Giselle, my new roomy'.

"Ohh! Hi, Giselle, see you later, I have to hurry, Nish greeted her and left. Both the girls entered the room, it was bright as the lights were on. Pointing to the left side bed Miach said, "That is your bed, your cupboard and your bureau". Remembering something, she continued, "Ohh! And that was Nish, a very good girl, but quote-unquote 'beware', she is no one's".

Giselle picked up her baggage and started keeping her meagre things in the cupboard and sat on her bed, from her baggage she removed a small mirror and kept it aside. She out of curiosity started enquiring about Nish, "Miach, wasn't she there with you at the entrance, when you were studying, where was she then? And she had your keys'. Miach a slow processor began pondering with her thumb in her mouth. Suddenly she with a loud voice, 'Yes, she wasn't, where was she then?' but was not earnest enough to find an answer too, dashed into the shower.

 Giselle picked up the mirror and closed her eyes, a mightily intense voice from the mirror spoke, 'Yes, my child, you have reached safe and sound' the voice continued, 'There was a visitor in your room in your absence, please scan the room'. Giselle again closed her eyes and opened the cage to let the tiny badger out, she said," Ninnus go!

Ninnus ran around with a glare of blue light from its eyes like a broad focus torch. The light was as blue as the sea, which scanned every corner of the room, suddenly the light flickered exactly at the window opposite to where Giselle's cot was kept, and the badger stopped. She picked the badger in her hand; pampered it and let it away and said," Good boy, off you, go" and top a hand full of nuts from her pocket and placed it in the badger cage, the badger hopped in, shutting the door behind.

She then went close to it to reveal a small red globe hemmed into the drape on the window. She closed her eyes to end the scan and crushed the stone after cutting it off the curtain.

 She returned to the mirror the voice was still there and it spoke again, 'Good work, I have full faith in you…, stay alert'.

Giselle winced dutifully blurting her heart out, 'Why me?...
can I...' again in a subdued tone, "Father, why me? ...
Why me...? She sobs....

Chapter 4-Advice and Hope

Giselle hesitant and unhappy as the sky would be falling on her, listened to the authoritarian voice as it spoke, 'There's a snitch in the group; a snoop of the mighty vicious, with the plot of what is to befall…'.
The voice rhythmically continued;

'Grief accelerated,

Pain initiated,

every soul to cry,

many abode to fly.

Wretched plans; wrath,

nipped the strength,

landings unknown

perdition or exoneration

Cherub; combat, mitigate

brace; in your joust

emancipate the anguish

glorify, for a panache

"But, father, how can I…?" said Giselle whimpering. Before she could complete, the voice said, "Ok, fair attention, my child, you are the only one, the creator has assigned, so be…" and the mirror instantly signs off with a flash, the next moment, the handlebar of the door twisted and swiftly jolted open as though earnestness did not want the conversation to end and to eavesdrop. The reckless audacity, she sensed and thought,' My father left, hmm…, no wonder', seeing Nish in front of her.

Nish stood before her; a lean lanky figure with lovely long hair, voluminous and tinted with sun-kissed blond halfway down the length. What captured Giselle's attention was her dare-devil eyes; which seemed like a portal--set to devour, a mighty red-eye scanner toiling hard, as she scanned through me and the room. Giselle was confused was it just a hunch, or is it she; the snitch in the group or the unprecedented!

Nish trying to deviate the gnawing looks of Giselle, said, "Hey Giselle, who were you talking to!"

Giselle, still in her trance of thoughts, jerked out saying, "Yeah, hi, no one…" suddenly the Badger purred and Giselle continued, "Ahh! That's my pet, I was talking to, she loves to hear me talk" paused and "Can I help you?"

Nish asked, "Where is Miach? I had to discuss some topics with her, as my exams are around the corner?' she continued, 'Where were you studying earlier?'. Just then Miach returned and said, 'Come, Giselle, let's go to the library".

They walked out of the room Nish seemed a little disappointed and continuously blabbered with Miach as they walked down the long corridor at the fag-end, Kanika was awaiting them, taking a shifty of the girls and summons the stairs.

The gorgeous stairs arrive and a voice resounds, "Where to gentle ladies?" Kanika commands, "Take us to the library". Swish the stairs move and the next moment, they were at the library.

As they walked down to the library hall, a splendour with three-level access. The reading hall with a high ceiling with crafted blocks inscribed and superscribed with magical spells and warfare instincts. Giselle read a few and thought,' Theses are trash'. The sky-blue ceiling with the box frames in gold and the huge lite crystal chandelier hanging from it contributed to the shimmery unstable undulations on the ceiling; mesmerizing, worth staring at. The hall placed straight and round tables with a powder-coated cobalt blue velvety finishing and French empire chairs upholstered in velvet and cotton fabrics with a mixture of highlighted blue and gold flowery print flanked the tables. Pedestal lamps stood from the floor at extreme ends every table in ones and twos to spotlight the tables. The hall was decorated with flowerpots and flowers from the lands of Michiana and terracotta pottery on the central tables or in glass cases.

At the centre of the hall was a huge see-through cylindrical glass fixed around the largest table. It was in focus from any corner of the library and vice-versa. The librarian was seated at a circular table or a platform around her with a revolving chair and there were a few students seated at the table engrossed in reading. Seeing Giselle, the librarian looked at her, 'Hello Giselle!' she said graciously, she continued,' Have you registered? come let me help". Giselle moved towards the table, though her eyes were still admiring the hall. The others moved up towards their levels and Giselle got busy with the librarian getting her formality completed.

Giselle securitized the place, she looked up to find the levels with the bookshelves decked in metallic cobalt blue colour with a dash of gold on the border frames, they were built from the floor to the ceiling awesomely bifurcated with panel paintings and cleverly disguised the books not revealed to the students. The shelves were stacked with books of the medieval era, a vast number of antiquarian books, and medical and scientific antique books written over centuries. Alluring ladders of threes and fours were suspended on each level, ultimately busy delivering books to the children. The 3rd level contained magical books as labelled on the railings visible from the floor of the hall, Giselle thought, she would go up there.

In the library, silence reigned except for the light murmur and the soothing aroma that floated in the air from the flowers in the pot, which permeated happiness and goodness. The diligent students of the university engrossed in their work were very appealing to watch.

Giselle explored the stairway to the third floor, one of the ladders saw her and rushed to her and exclaimed, 'At your service, madam!' She answered, 'Vironanomaterialoh Therapy book' the ladder signed with its arm and swung across for the book, it was one of the hidden books in the panel. The librarian alerted looked up and then eased and continued working realizing it was Giselle.

She approached her friends and settled with them and began discussing certain features in the book as it revealed only what the students could read.

As Giselle was involved in the conversation, she got edgy because of her endeavoured snare of Nish and tried escaping it. She gained confidence and thoughts brewed in her mind,' Watch out, the powers and virtue will entangle. The murky mist has cleared off my mind alerting me; beware, she had sneaked into my room to fix the red globe. Intentions-it burdened was foiled'. Suddenly, the friendly ladder appeared with a thick book and said' Here child, the book you had asked for' and instantly shinned away.

After an hour or so the huge frame hanging at the entrance is visible from every corner of the library,

The message was followed by an image, the librarian and Mr Warbhinger, who was also there at that movement stood up in accordance, when they saw Sir Prakinasus. Miach instantly got up thrilled, she abruptly blurted, 'My dad'

The image began speaking, "Hail Marjodarna! Glory to King Puissant! Hail the young Caloth Militia! how are you all?" After a pause the image continues, "This announcement is to inform and alert you, as the watchtowers have been decoding unusual disturbances in the Cloth area. Disquietude amongst the trees and the transpire of the white-winged horse has been spotted. I fear, it has probably instilled some pestilent life, which may be anomalous for all".

'Hail Marjodarna! Hail king Puissant!' "Stay safe"

The frame signs off with a flash, an air of distress and apprehension begins to gather in the hall. While the children ambled away anxious, the relentless roguish stare of Nish fixed on Giselle continued, Nish was disturbed but by what…? Was it the beauty Giselle was attracted or was it something…?

Dolefully, perplexed, Giselle got up and quietly rambled off, unnoticed with the book.

A while later, Himu and Thino came up to them, "Howz it going?" and then looking at Miach, Himu asked,' Well then, where is your roomy?' he continued with loaded sarcasm to the other pointing at Miach, 'Ha ha ha, already abandoned her'. All of them chortled amused. Miach banged the table out of fury.

Nish to deviate their attention and to get some info asked Himu, 'Did you hear the announcement Miach's dad made?'

Himanshu replied, "No, what is it? I wasn't here",

The next moment, Miach perceiving something shoved back the chair, which went shooting back and bellowed," Himu, come, let's go look for Giselle", she continued, "Come, I will tell you as we look for her, she was right here with us…" she continued, 'My father will kill me".

Himu agreed, "Me too" With a grave look that envisaged his face, he hurried behind Miach.

By then the children around got frantic as Giselle was new and did not know the auberge well, they thought she could, or probably would get lost. Panic-struck, they all started dispersing helter-skelter looking for her.

A grave sense of responsibility and apprehension enveloped Himu's and Miach's faces, as they headed towards the entrance…

Chapter 5-The Oracle

The children in the hall procrastinated for a while and began murmuring and discussing, 'Who is Giselle? Who is she?'…

Nish stood there glued and agitated with Thino and Miso, trying hard to figure out what her next move could be. Perplexed to where they could find her, both dashed to the entrance and Himu summoned the stairs and, in a jiffy, they were gone.

Nish stood there with her confidants, affixed, contemplating ways to accomplish their skirmish contrivance. On the third floor, Himu and Miach terror-struck frantically were looking for her, Miach had conveyed to Himu the announcement and he was well aware of the tenacious and unrelentless foe clouding over them.

The winged horse was drudgery, agony and pain, 'Mankind to suffer from famine, fire, sickness and death' 'It could turn to a time of agony and pain', he thought. The thought of it, itself shrilled through his spine and hastily moved in search of Giselle.

In the library, Giselle, as she moved towards the entrance of the library in a confused state, a turmoil of thoughts lashed her mind, continuously plotting the patterns to deal with.

She thought: her army; her counterparts and no postulation conceived, she thought, 'Miach, would be with me, I guess'.. She continued her murmuring, "Who else, father, what… what next', then exclaimed, 'The garden…,". Her incessant thoughts embodied the perils that lay instore, which got intervened as she paused. She jerked stopped and her head bent downwards, her eyes caught sight of two boots standing in front, unanticipatedly, she would have collided into the figure, she instantly looked up and Mr Warbhinger stood in front of her.

 "You are beckoned, please join me to the garden", Mr Warbhinger's raucous voice resounded. The directive and instructional voice sent a wave of thought again rippling in her mind, 'Who has summoned me? Has father appeared…,' 'No', she thought, 'He wouldn't, it is too early for him…; and her mind clouded with trivial and less significant thoughts? Slowly she followed him, as he signalled the stairs and both vanished into thin air!

At the hostel, Miach and Himu arriving on the third floor rushed to Miach's room; it was still locked, flummoxed at the turn of events, Miach points her finger at the lock. The handle twist and the door screeching at intervals opens slowly, Miach looks at the door and says, 'Hush', the creaking stops, and they rush in only for the dismay of the absence of Giselle. Disappointed, Himu hits the recliner in the room and slumped into it, watched over by Miach as she sat gazing at her bed.

 Miach, "What do you think? Where could she be? "

 "What do we do, now? Where do we look for her?" Himu uttered indistinctly downhearted.

Silence and anxiety proliferated in the room, Miach bit her nail tips as though she had a task in hand of eradicating it. It was a while that the two had been thinking and suddenly, disrupting the serenity, Miach sprang to her legs with a snap, she hollered, 'The garden'. Himu also swung into action and both of them began exiting the room. The attempt was foiled as Nish barged into the room, fathoming her deliberate appearance accompanied by her confidants, Thino and Miso. Little were they aware of the evil intentions of Nish, that she was to scotch the possible assistance to Giselle by hindering the exit or probably house arresting Himu and Miach in the chamber.

Tino and Miso stood at the door, while Nish installed herself on Giselle's bed and began talking, "Miach, today professor Mr Livesprinsus tried to introduce… "and she went jibber-jabbering on and on. She tried jumping topics, vomiting lame jokes to engage, entertain and keep them from leaving.

Mr Warbhingsus and Giselle appeared in the garden; a strange hue of blue glow infused the front yard to form a backdrop to what was to be witnessed, light seemed to radiate from every flower of the stephanotis Debbie plant. The white flowers radiated in blue, as though suspiring for a message to deliver. Every inch of the garden seemed living; it exuded an air of tranquillity, the leaves and branches still as though ordained with strict instructions. She stepped down the mighty stairs onto the pathway; the tortuous, ill-defined and ragged serpentine strip of the pathway toiled laboriously setting itself to pave a smooth and undeterred walk. The shrivelled twigs, the leaves desiccated orange and the greens seemed to tiptoe out of the craggy path. The verdure of shrubs and weeds with violets and crimsons; all in attendance as in a parade, looked up towards Giselle and turned their heads as she moved, as though glorifying an ennoble presence.

The white flowers radiated in blue with an urgency to deliver a message and an impromptu whispering followed. As she moved on the pathway followed by Mr Warbhinger, a pink-tinged cloud spread thwarted a lean figure awaiting her. She was daunted at first, which was supported by Mr Warbhinger, as the figure was very tall, her flowy gown was not touching the floor, it swayed feebly and her cape with strips of stroll swayed in the air. She thought 'Something uncontrollable had taken its ultimate turn and has cast its detrimental frigate, it will doom the sphere of living, Alas! Her gorge raised, she tried to swallow hard, her face drooped down its bloom to a despondent pale. She walked ahead as her ears attract faint voices but does not yield to the hearing, she continues to saunter towards the damsel, her thoughts gauging, she must be, no! she is one of the tree nymph-ornamentals at the fountain', 'Yes, indeed, she is' 'ahh! They are...' she continued as the others soon appeared behind her. They were beautiful and mesmerizing and part of the platoon of her father, each with its strength and a whole army.

Himu and Miach sensing the cruel undertone in Nish's strange behaviour managed to dodge her with Kanov entering the scene and taking control of Nish, she outsmarted and took Nish off-guard with her colours of purple and grey cast on them. And there; Nish and her escorts forgot why they were there and began indulging with Kanov the charmer. Himu and Miach wasted no time flew out of the chamber and hurried down as guessed by

Miach.

As Giselle approached the figure, it suddenly split into two others from behind to flank the damsel in pink, and began speaking in chorus:

"Hail Regina Puella Giselle, The Fortis! Daughter of the Great Puissant, the protector of the realm, the Salvator!."Accept our greeting! We are here with the nuntius of the Oracle! Instantly, a low echoing of the word 'Oracle' 'The Oracle' 'Giselle' began to surge in the background. The Nymphs continue: "Danger befalls, the far east torment and wail, winged that spot. Vermin disguised, life; the man at price inferno strikes, sons of Nyx conspire. Exasperated mourns, Thanatos transpire holocaust; extinction, Hypnos entice Cherub naïve, valiant and resolute authentic stephanotis; steer, aide. Cherub; you lead, comrade to guide follow you; warriors to fade. Heartfelt, lion-hearted confront souls to cast, to the eupnea last. (The damsels Pause and slow down with a heavy heart, they continued) Triumph; glory be you spread

The holocaust, incur to shed.Cherub, yours' the most, know not the rest!

The damsel pauses and again, "The nuntius too hard but we with you all along"

Himu and Miach had just arrived and barged out of the entrance towards the garden, they were awestruck by the picturesque scenario and the instant outcome of events. They began descending the steps not believing their eyes and wearily plodded towards Giselle; pacified as they assumed they were on time.

Miach and Himu run towards Giselle, as she breaks down sobbing and wailing, "Why me… father? I am so meek and frail, how will I? she sits with her head buried in her palms bent onto her elevated knees. Miach and Himu unaware of anything try to console her. They were not able to understand as it was not clear, what the flowers were repeatedly saying. Stephanotis Debbie flowers were garrulously blabbering 'Regina Puella Giselle', 'fortis', 'Hail Magna Rex Dias' and 'Oracle' the tone repeated like a stuck record pin went into a screaming mode, when...

Suddenly, the spectacle falls flat, there is dead silence and the lapsed aura and the garden resumes normalcy. The nymphs disappeared and the flowers stopped singing. Stunned, the three looked up and looked around, as they turned back in a moment, they could see Nish with her accomplice rushing out of the building towards them...

Chapter 6-The Null before the storm

The extravaganza from the shrubs to the pine tops dropped as a fall of the fountain, the starlets disappeared, violets to the damsels reversed and the glorifying blooms reduce to their shrunk dehydrated state… The parading ceased, the resonance of the Stephanotis' paused and started a coarse soft rumbling as though the record pin revolted, the murmuring of the starlets and the wind smoothened to breeze passing soothingly and pleasant. The magnitude of strength and display of the hegemonic power that proclaimed and professed the doom attenuated and faded abruptly, leaving behind doubt and uncertainty. The whole scenario transited into an enigmatic trance and it was pitch dark again; no moon showed to shed its light to uncover the penumbra. The enchantment and the eminence faded off leaving no residue behind for the virtuoso sorceress…

Nish appeared at the entrance; she saw Miach and hastily scampered down the steps to her asking, "What happened? she incoherently urged and tried to indulge them. She coaxed and shuddered Himu several times to reply.

Himu's silence did not break but thought, 'Why is Nish so desperate?... why?'; Is she the Marionette or is she…? Suddenly a tense perplexity overlapped Himu's face as he always had a soft corner for Nish, he grew anxious and was eager to leave the garden with Giselle.

Probably, Himu also felt his hopes thwarted by the revelation of the moment and stifled by the revulsion it will follow. He rushed towards Giselle with a sudden sense of responsibility but again got confronted by Nish, she pulled him towards her and again demanded in a very seductive manner, "Won't you tell me what has happened?" All her means to extract what just happened were in vain, however hard she tries.

Nish tried deviating her expression for a favourable and concerned one, "Oh! You found her" "Where was she? Is she hurt?" she continued relentlessly. Himu; ignored her as he had his doubts, and continued with a cold shoulder. He did not want to disappoint her, but somewhere in his mind rang a bell 'You are doomed'.

 Himu was one of Nish's favourites or probably her crush, this behaviour started vexing her, which was no acceptance for her. But for Himu, what next was muddling him and all that Nish said did not bank on him. Himu was always enticed by Nish and her beauty, while she took advantage of it or probably, she also was attracted to him. Now she feels threatened with the onset of a new name 'Giselle'

Miach on hearing the rattling said," No, she is fine, she just tripped and twitched her limb" she was concentrating on Giselle and hardly heeded the bothersome queries of Nish. Miach headed as if she had been assigned a task and continued, "Give way let me take Giselle to her room" contemptuously dismissed the demand and helped Giselle by her shoulders and both feebly walked towards the entrance.

Nish daunted back and stood there baffled, although she had tried to get updated on what was happening. She was a little distressed and hurried behind them to the hostel.

As they entered the hallway, Thino standing there pulled Nish jerking her towards him, "Hey, what happened to your investigation; why do you look so baffled?" questioned Thino and remarked with a pause "He; your Himu is with the newcomer, haha…" with loaded sarcasm he continued, "What is so great about her, she is so just 'OK' and no comparison to you". "Is she your next challenge?"

"Hush! Nothing curious about her: Can you shut up and follow me?" retorted Nish. And she mumbled, "What are they in a hurry for, there is still time…"

"Time…time for what?" Thino astonished exclaimed "Time for what, you are creeping me out. Please can you …" before he could continue Miso pounced on him and grabbed covered his mouth to shut, "Hushshhhh! There is someone out there" Miso whispered. Miso heard some hustle behind him and looked back, he seemed to see a shadow standing behind them, instantly he turned shuddered and moved at a quicker pace.

Complete silence prevailed, the nocturnes also stopped their weird creaks and screeches, as Miso saw a silver-lined shadow move past … Miso looked back as the sounds recommenced after some time, there was nothing and thought 'oh… you are scared of what… fear not; she is here and she is very kind' and gradually they moved into their habitats.

 At the hostel, Nish did not share her room with anyone. She did not have a roomy though an extra bed shared her room. That night before the dinner call, Thino and Miso were seen frequently in and out of Nish's room. A treacherous transitional saga seemed to be brewing in her room. Mummering with intermittent mirthful laughter diffused in and around her chamber, it seemed to envelop the machination behind the dark drapes of treachery. Was Nish the sorceress or is she merely a marionette as suspected by Himu. What was it? Or just another warrior of the Neptunians.

Miso, famished opened the door to go to the dining hall, and felt intimidated and slid back, as he saw the shadow with the silver line standing at the door and pushing itself into the room and vanished. Miso without informing left the room. announcement for dinner could be heard and the presence of the

students flooded the corridor. In the next few minutes, the doors of the hostel chambers invariably flung open and shut to get the corridor noisy. Students were seen bustling off through the corridors to the stairways and the babbling echoed. Miso also pushed himself out terrified and blend into the crowd.

Nish and Thino also gushed out of the chamber and the next moment they were at the entrance of the dining hall.

"Ahh...! the dining- one of my favourite places'" said Nish "I feed on … "

Thino, "what happened? A change in your tone" "never mind".

The dining hall is an exorbitant room with a crescent-shaped table topped with tinted silver framed glass. Each had a seating of twelve: seven on one side and five on the opposite with exquisite wooden chairs lined with silver borders and Arabian carved back supports, upholstered with fine Chinese silk and velvet. A crescent-shaped smaller size chandelier made of zirconium crystals hung over each table providing ample lighting to the diners. The tables were topped with food served in porcelain and glassware. The cutlery with fine German silver was well-polished and food was mounted on a rotatory table mounted. The wine was served in the silver brimmed goblet set aside for each dish. Swish swash churned the rotator as the children began taking their share of serve.

 Nish stood there pleased as she started reading the thought of those present there. 'Who is that new girl…', 'I wish to befriend her…', 'she looks like a damsel' 'Mr Warbhinger looks very keen to help her…' 'The food is yum today… hey! someone is reading our thoughts" and so on, a tsunami of thought overwhelmed her mind when suddenly she heard, 'I wish I knew what was the lighting outside this evening, it was very conspicuous and wish I was a part of it' Nish's gaze instantly went looking for the owner of the thoughts, she travelled with the thoughts, which went hither thither probably moving with the food but before she could reach it became silent.

'Who was it that who had witnessed what had happened? Nish thought, 'I wish I could find it'

Nish waited for the thoughts to resurface but nothing happened, probably got warned. She looked around if Miach and Himu were around, but none of them had arrived for dinner. She raged at Thino, "How much will you eat? It will show up all over your body as lumps" and left keen to know where the group was and a little frantic. Thino hushed up the dinner disappointed and followed her. Thino thought,' What is with her? sometimes I feel to move on' Instantly, Nish turned back and gave a stern look at Thino, she waved her fingers and said," Not possible Thino, we will return for dinner as I'm also hungry" His thoughts were read. Nish again said, "let's take a stroll in the hostel"

She thought 'It's dead silent why? Where are they? What if…'

Chapter 7-The Colours of Kanov

In the corridor, Kanov is spotted strolling in the passage restless, anxious; the passage infused with an array of colours, creating an aura- yes! She reflects her conscience; her thoughts send the vibrating colours around her. Colours began permeating into the atmosphere, which changed from orange to a subtle yellow tinged with white, gradually outlining the yellow with the thought of hope that faded away and then to purple, which got darker from the lighter as anxious she got; she was jittery, of course! She had a hunch of the unprecedented and went out to warn the others, but they were not anywhere to be seen.

'Where did all of them go? Why was I not informed of this venture?' racked her mind. 'It would be a catastrophe if I don't stop them' she thought. Kanov went on pacing up and down the corridor unaware of what has been seasoned by the group. When Nish and Tino prop up into the corridor all of a sudden, Nish yells,' It's purple: don't go", and pulls Tino back, "Apprehension has flustered her mind, she is dangerous, keep off'. The next moment, she thought, 'Why was she anxious? Where are the others?' Is something cooking? Ohh! My Himu! She gasps.

Nish began to premeditate with all the assumptions and spite for Giselle, 'Oh! That wretched Giselle, she has just ruined our friendship and relationship'. She jolts her head up to the sky and mutters harshly, "Did you know this?

Why do you have to do it now…? Why! Tino was surprised; perplexed, "What did you just say and to whom? Nish shuns him saying, 'Nothin!... come let's go'. They both exit through the hallway unnoticed by Kanov.

Kanov, still in the passage, slowly moves towards Nish's room with the cloud following her slowly fading and pauses at the door and lends her ears to the room door to perceive if there was any movement there. But in vain attempts at any gain, suddenly she hears footsteps hurling towards her and the cloud instantly disappears. A bunch of young learners pass her frolicking. They stopped their loud prattle and smiled, waving at her. Kanov fondly returns the wave and gradually drifts away into the brightness of the hallway.

Where and what was the group up to?

Nish and her stooges returned to the dining hall, which was still loud and bustling with the chattering of the children enjoying their sumptuous alimentation. Children clutched their compartmental dishes filled with a variety of food and darted toward their tables. Nish got onto a table and with a finger twitch, shooed away the young boys seated there. The juniors with the fear of the seniors just scampered and found someplace for themselves.

Nish, as she took her place on one of the chairs near the table, scanned every nook and corner of the dining room to lock in Himu or members of his group.

Nish tapped on the table rhythmically with her five fingers, 'Tino, do you have an idea where the group is? She asked not to find them in the room. Where do you …? She continued just then Miso charged at them panting and stammering," Nish… Nish!"

Ufff!!! What Nish! Can you please go ahead"?

Miso continued, "They!... The group was seen heading towards the human habitats". Nish starts up from her chair "Really, where, who…?" She was perplexed and excited and continued "Ohh! That is why Kanov was anxious, hmmm…" "Now, I get it, she does not know where they are… gotcha!"

"I will let the cat out tomorrow, for Sure!" She said "And … let's go for the surgical strike and see the pickles splattered around" she hopped off her chair with a murky smile and dashed towards the service counter. Both her associates followed her.

Miso, 'But dinner, I am so hungry. Let's eat!!

Nish, 'You eat! I am full of the news you brought, thank you. She turns to Thino, 'Come Thino, let's do some homework for the excitement tomorrow" she pulls him by his T-shirt and drags him towards the door. At the door, Thino rebuffed him, pulling himself free, 'I want to have dinner, I 'll come later" he said. Both of them stay back to enjoy their dinner.

Nish released him and mocked, 'OK, run-on with your dinner, worthless as you are, I have work to do" she pauses and continues satirically 'Lots of work!!!

Before midnight, Nish returned to her room but on her way, as she passed Giselle's room, she stopped to eavesdrop at the door but it was silent, a silence like an indrawn breath; silence like the null before the storm.

Chapter 8-The Boy in the Hood

Earlier in the evening, the group sat at the fireplace in Giselle's room, when Miach said, "I am bored now and exhausted, can we sneak into our stamping ground?".

Himu replied harshly, 'No, no, no…, it is dangerous" paused for a moment" Don't you remember the announcement yesterday…, I am not going anywhere"

Earlier in the day, three others joined the group after they saw Giselle and closely followed them. They were Abratos, whom they called the undaunted as his name, Celosia and Damyan. Damyan was a calm and timid boy, who was the controller in calmness, while Celosia would be defined soon. A very slim figure with long brown hair, which she loved tinting blonde on half the length from the bottom. Her bouncy silky hair and her bewitching beauty always attracted the boys, hmmm…! I guess Nish was jealous of her too.

The three grabbed the opportunity to voice their sortie or were they assigned to reach there at that time not sure. Was Giselle building an army for herself or was she assigned with some mission unprecedented to the others?

The group continued their discussion, Giselle was quiet and calm, When Himu and Damyan also said, "It could be trouble". Instantly Celosia got up with a little irritation and mouthed, "Why, I am also bored, let's go".

The group looked at Giselle and in chorus, "Can we?"

Abratos, said, 'I will only if Giselle is in'. Giselle shook her head in acknowledgement. They prepared to leave, it was almost dark, and a little apprehension was visible on Giselle's face. All of them took their cycles, Giselle shared it with Himu as he offered one and left the gates.

It was a no moon night and pitch dark except for the light from the star and the floodlights from the cycles, slowly the cycles picked up to the skies, and Giselle could feel the warmth and the aroma of the flowers touch her inner self trying to suppress the uncertainty in her. The flowers had started emitting the fragrance of courage and a few others with calmness as they had sensed the turmoil in Giselle. Giselle enjoyed the ride with the soft gentle breeze embracing her slowly the cycle began to descend and they were on the ground, after a while it stopped.

Himu led the group, he said 'Anoixe! Anoixe! Anoixe!' to a group of trees.

In the next movement, a voice said, "Eísai sígouros"

Himu replied," Nai"

The next moment a rumbling could be heard and the trees vanished, and the lights of the human inhabitants and the high-rise buildings well-lit could be seen. As they passed through the street, the rumbling of the vehicles and the honking deafened Giselle. She said, "It is so noisy and loud". She could feel the chill as fall was close. She asked Him" Do you frequently come here?. Himu nodded no for an answer.

Himu replied a little that this is how humans live, they don't care about any pollution, and they do not realise the harm it does to nature and their very existence. They harm for their benefit and luxury. They explore what is not for them".

He continues with a very soft and almost fragile voice, "They fight for land, where land never grabs for land…"

He continues after some time "Land that does not belong to them, they bring metals and chemical weaponry to fight for it and shed their blood in the name of land". He continues with a heavy voice as though his heart mourns, "My heart sores up when I think our Earth is so humble that a part of her does not ask for the other part, the whole globe lives in harmony, and she has to bear all the misuse of humans on her, just because she is the mother". He pauses and becomes silent. He continues, "We defend them for their policies, we save them from the wrath of nature, I pity ourselves that we are bound...", Himu abruptly stops as he hears the calls from behind.

Miach and Celosia come behind them and asked," Where are we going? Do you have any Idea, Himu" Himu"? He stops as the other approach the group, Abratos 'Do you have a place in your mind?'

" Yes, we go to our stamping ground" Himu continues," It was a very calm and cosy place"

"Yes, a fun place and the food was Yum!" exclaimed Damyan 'come, let go'.

They all went on the road to the beautiful restaurant called 'To Nkourmé or 'The gourmet'. The restaurant has a grand ambience well-lit with various colour shades and a valet dressed in a Greek costume and a lady at the reservation table where you need to reserve the table. It has ample parking space for cars and flying cycles. It has rooftop parking for avionacars or flying cars. Inside was a little shady with dim lights and the attendant would guide you to the reserved table with a torchlight.

As they reached the restaurant, they headed to the reservation counter, but as they parked the cycles, they looked around to find the parking lot almost empty. Himu looked around and thought, 'Why is this parking lot empty today? It is the weekend for the humans' which distracted him a little but then overcame it soon.

Damyan got the reservation done and the attendant soon approached them at the entrance and guided them with his torch and took them to their table. It was dark as they entered, except for the spotlight looking down nothing else was visible. Slowly the room was visible and the band began to play, Giselle was flabbergasted by the magnificence of the hall and gradually the architecture emanated leaving her agape.

Abratos garrulously went on talking and cracking lame jokes entertaining the group, while Giselle admired the place. She scanned through the tables and the arrangements, abruptly, her eyes spotted a boy sitting in a hood at a table diagonally opposite to where she was seated. She sensed that he was looking at her, but dropped his head as she looked at him. She waited for him to look up, but in vain, when the small light amidst his fingers caught her attention. He had some blue electric connection manifested in his fingers and then faded away the next second. She waited for him to show himself, just the Miach jerked her hand," Giselle, what will you drink?" she continued, "What happened? check the menu to order". Passing her the menu booklet.

Giselle, "Miach, please order the same as for yourself, it is fine with me" saying so she looked for the boy in the hood, astonishingly he had disappeared, with the glass of drink just left unfinished.

Giselle thought to herself, 'Maybe, I just assumed 'she lifted the glass of water to drink, when she receives mind waves, "Hello Giselle!"
"What..., who... how...?' Giselle recognises the thought and stunned, drops the glass in her hand...

Chapter 9-The Brawl

The tumbler crash-landed on the floor with a big band. Giselle stood up and looked around but could not see anyone. Miach and Himu slid out of their chairs towards Giselle as she stood dumbstruck. They tried to coax her to know, what had happened but Giselle was silent.

Giselle, "It's nothing," with a pause she continued, "I… I thought, I heard someone, let it be we shall continue, where is the order?" Though she spoke her mind was cloudy and her eyes desperate and anxiously searching. Himu sensed that something is going wrong and he kept a watch.

The music changed and went on to a fast number. "Isn't that 'footloose, ohh! I have always loved the number", Said Celosia. Miach signalled Abratos, asking him for a dance. Abratos instantly sprung out of his place and they both started Jive dancing near the table. The others watched them gleefully and intermittently, Himu also jumped into the act and invited Giselle to join.

The enjoyment abruptly ceased, as a commotion could be heard at the entrance. The squabble had picked up the pitch that the music stopped and a few attendants could be seen running towards the door.

Hearing the commotion, Himu signalled the group to leave, as the children were about to, two of the waiters were flung into the restaurant. Four or five men appeared entering the restaurant, Himu said," Stay alert and still! We don't want trouble" before he could finish the light of the restaurant came bright and one of the fellows, who must be over six feet tall came darting to them. The man was young and he came towards Giselle and touched Celosia on her back and left.

The others followed him and did similar perversions, while one of them with a red scarf around his neck bent down towards Giselle, air-kissed her and took hold of a lock of her hair and left smoothly passing them through his fingers. Giselle's face grew pale as the last man whispered in her ears, "I will get you!".

Himu asked a waiter, who these people were, for which the waiter replied that one was a local goon and constantly pestered, while the other four were new. Miach, who was calm and quiet had a turmoil of rage brewing in her. Damyan the gentle, watched Miach fuming up, so he sneaked his hands into her palm and held it tight, calming her down to quench the raging fire. He was very well aware of the consequence. On the contrary, the action of Abratos took Damyan by surprise as Abratos sprung from his chair and confronted the last man with the red scarf on his way.

Abratos grimly said," Yes, mister what do you think you are doing" keeping his hand on the man's chest. The man sent a stern look at Abratos, which undeterred him, and said, "Buzz off!" pushing him away. Abratos went flying and crashed into the table nearby. The man looked at Giselle as a rebuke, which flinched her and she quietly sat down. Himu and Miach instantly signalled the others to head out. They had not ordered, but tipped the waiter and left the hall.

As they swiftly moved out, Himu held Giselle's hand and began maundering 'We had been to this place several times, nothing happened. What is it now"? Celosia asked Giselle," What is it with that man and you, Giselle? Do you know him?" Giselle nodded in denial.

The group stepped out to be astounded to see the men-a set of the jeering mob was already there. They were belittling and taunting the group. Himu and his friend tried to avoid the contemptuous ridicule and moved toward their cycles. One of the men came towards Miach and kicked her cycle, which broke Miach's resistance and took him by his neck and hurled him with all her might to the floor, where the man fell on his back with a thud. All the others approached them in a jiffy and encircled them in the next movement.

Himu gave cover to Giselle and confronted them, the man with the red scarf started beating up Himu with blows around his chest and stomach. Himu was defensive and also tried kicking the man and strangling him with his feet. On the other side, the rest of them also picked up a fight, while Giselle clung to one of the pillars of the parking area. and succumbed to the fight, terror-struck and helpless. Miach picked up the fight and soon could overcome one of the goons, who fell but suddenly disappeared. Himu who saw that suddenly got up with all his might while the others were all beaten up to half their life and shouted "Run! Run! Take to your cycles ", Himu shouted and turned to Giselle, "Run! get to Miach" "Go!"

Giselle started running towards Miach, who was waiting to grab her hands, intermittently turning back to Himu, when the man with the scarf pounced from nowhere and grabbed Giselle by her hair and started dragging her.

Giselle tried to free herself but the pace was fast enough that they had got off the foot and were lifted from the ground. The movement the man in the scarf got hod of Giselle all the others vanished. The group started running behind them but lacked energy and fell back.

As the man rose and laughed to glorify his victory and belittled Himu and his group, Himu began running in the direction trying to pull Giselle down, what happened next surprised all of them, a ball of light struck him and the rising got deactivated and rapidly came down. Giselle saw the boy in the hood right in front of them and muttered 'Harshinus'.

She thought, 'How has he appeared?' Giselle struggled to set herself free; when a thump on the man's back pushed him to fall flat on his face and let Giselle free. Giselle looked back to see -the damsels in action, of which one of the damsels spoke, "Are you hurt?" Giselle just whimpered and nodded for a no.

The boy in the hood also came down and was ready with his hand lifted apart as all the vanished men started appearing one by one. By the time Himu could reach them, the boy had pulled energy from nature. There was uncommon flanging of the roaring tremble and a thunderous sound, crackling flashes combined like a whirlpool into his arms. All the trees around him seemed to be transferring data from him with the quivering of the leaves and dehydrating rapidly.

Giselle started running towards the cycles, by then the atmosphere had built up with the trees sending their leaves and short tree barks sharply at the men that darted like missiles to cut, to bleed. The street and the sky reverberated with the intense pressure and sound. The men saw the damsels and one of them said: "Run! The boy is deadly!". But the boy had already built up the energy that went like a magnetic wave that dropped two of them instantly dead. The showering of leaves continued as it continued at 100 to 120 kilometres per hour. The dry twigs pierced the body and the men began wailing in pain. They were disappearing partially as the boy's powers were not letting them leave. Two others were pinned to the ground while being tormented by the waves from the hooded boy attracted their body fluids were attracting afflicting pain, the men were shuddering and howling in pain. The group was running towards the spectacle, while Giselle started running towards them. One of the men started chasing Giselle, slowly he was floating as though he was air surfing. The man started growing in size as he approached and the huge thing darted towards Giselle but was obstructed by one of the damsels, who followed Giselle as she was running. The thing fell back to normal as the nymph started throwing magical blows, which were inflicting wounds all over his body, sharp twigs started piercing him and the leaves passed him cutting his skin all over. The nymph faded as she saw the group coming towards them and stayed there with Giselle invisible, while Himu and Miach ran to help the boy.

As they got closer, Miach flung the concatenate-demrrihe' toward the men, who were fighting with the boy. The men instantly crippled by it were bound by her string. The distraction of the hooded boy helped the other two men, who were pinned down by his mind powers and were continuously attacked by the trees get free and begin running into the forest. Himu starts chasing the men, he forced them to slow down with his powers, and as he approached them, he asked "Why are you after Giselle?" Himu continued" She is just a simple girl". Giving one of them a tight slap he continued," What do you want?". One of the men scoffed and the other gave a smirky smile and said, "You will soon", Himu was irritated by their audacity even as in captivity, on the verge to cast a spell on them to disintegrate their existence, when one of them yelled, 'To the stairs!" pointing to the right. One of the men kicked Himu, who was off guard and ran towards a staircase structure in the woods, Himu stumbled back to his feet and started chasing, Miach and Abratos also came running to the stairs only to see the men climb up the stairs and take a plunge. All the three followed the men up the stairs and found nothing other than what looked like an old abandoned staircase built amidst the woods and nothing else around it, where did they dive to.

Himu turned around to return to the crippled men and look for the boy in the hood, who had disappeared to his astonishment and thought,' What is happening?

Miach," We had to take them to the university, right!" "Do you think we are in trouble"?

"Yes", muttered Himu anxiously.

Before they could wrap up the scene, there was a flash of lightning in the sky and they saw the white-winged horse in the air. In a fraction of seconds, the rider hurled a string bright as light at the bound men and airlifted them dragging them to mid-air and vanished.

A sudden rumble of the gushing wind like the curtain had fallen and everything was back to normal; the music from the restaurant could be heard at a distance and people around were normally passing by. All of them petrified ran towards their cycles, Miach and Himu had used their powers, while the others had got beaten up. None of them wanted the night to give up to dawn as they had trespassed and done the unlawful. They wanted the night to elongate and to recuperate their wounds, fetch time to find excuses for what had been done.

As the cycles soared up, Giselle looked back as though her eyes were yearning…

Chapter 10-Reprimance

The morning at the university was a little exhausting, with the fear and chariness drill. last night's act conveyed to the authorities resonated throughout the university. The students were put to task with the abilities they were good at; their prudence was judged and reprimanded by the whip in command and at every error that lashed their backs. Little were the students aware of what the inducement was, of this turn of events. There was a sense of commotion and Chinese whisper in the air, while the drill followed with the timeworn lectures from their mentors, with the stare and raised brows that shuddered the children. They had intermittent visits from Sir Prakinasus and constantly gave motivated lectures in turns. The students, who witnessed the baleful unprecedented scuffle that passed last night; were summoned questioned and cross-questioned. They were under the scanner for their lenient attitude despite the announcement at the hostel and the university on the portending fear.

At the university, the hustle-bustle of the students intensified in the activity area, air whispered on the first floor outside the principal's office. The air rumbled and grumbled, and outlined into the nymphs until Giselle was summoned inside today. She was as quiet as an anchor in a dead calm, while they all stood in front of the door as quiet as the dark, without the slightest deflection of the pupils. All stood staring gloatingly, Giselle stood without the slightest remorse but with a little perplexity. What was it that was hindering her- the oracle hinted; not comprehendible by anyone? Suddenly, the silence broke and the door slammed open, out propped Mr Agafya's secretary and commanded harshly" You all are summoned". They entered the chamber to see Mr Agafya and Mr Charalambous seated in front and with their expressions posed the question, 'What happened?' The children started relating to the sequence of what transpired. There was an attempt to convince them of which they failed miserably. They were constantly rebuked by Mr Charalambous, constantly yelling and disturbed.

Mish and Himu pinned on to justify the state of Giselle; but perplexity conceived their minds, which would be hard for Giselle to convince in the long run, but time will take its turn. She was well aware of the questions posed by Mr Agafya and Mr Charalambous, yet she chose to keep quiet and continued to stand calm and still. This infuriated Mish and Himu; fingers pointed at Giselle, she stood there with her head bowed with no words to justify.

Mish began ranting about the incident, she said it was not her mistake the clump came in all of a sudden into the restaurant and blew into Gizelle hair. One of them with a red scarf brushed her shoulder and commented 'New one… eh! And she continued, "With an expression of smacking her, he went on "Very tasty, I guess, eh! ". She continued that he had said something else in her ear.

They had tried leaving the restaurant and the place as Himu had sensed some trouble. By then it was late, they followed to the parking and the brawl began. Without leaving her breath, she continued "This; sir, what outraged

Abratos and me, and we stepped in to teach him a lesson, little did we know what was in store and Giselle would be the reason for the chaos".

'Teach him a lesson! And why blame Giselle?" Roared Mr Chlaralambous, "Who do you think you are, and how dare you pick a fight in the human habitat! do you know the consequence?" He lifted himself from the chair, he had grown a little large and flung himself on the children. Mr Agafya was a little ruffled as Mr Chlaralambous crossed his sizing limit. Next, he again furiously thwacked his desk and at the thump, the pen stand, his nameplate and the papers on it bounced and settled back quickly as a wink. It looked as if the elements on the table also were tense and discombobulated.

The children were intimidated by the sudden turn of a sober and calm interrogation; to a harsh authoritative behest. They had never seen him like this, Mr Chlaralambous was considered the calmest and most composed professor and this was a change of facet. Mr Agafya got up from where he was seated and quietly watched the scenario, came close to Mr Chlaralambus, calmed him by patting him, which reduced Mr Chlaralambus to normal and slowly moved towards the door gentle as he is. Holding the door open, he turned towards others and said, "I think, it is time we hushed this up and be warned of what has to be done and also take the drills seriously" and left the room closing the door behind him.

In the corridor, he saw Nish standing behind the pillar, and asked if she also was part of the tiff. Nish shook her head for a 'no' and stood there like an ignorant silly cat. Mr Agafya was pretentious and knowing her intentions harshly asked her to buzz off. Nish sneaked her way behind the beam walls of the construction and rushed into the room just to her horrific revelation that all had left that was empty. She stumped her foot on the floor and roared 'Damn!'. She darts back to the library to meet Miss Schemoni.

At the library, as she steps in, Thino suddenly comes running, slides and drifts towards her, would trip a fall, but manages his balance and gives her the news of what had happened the last night. He relates the story, to his knowledge, in bits and pieces.

Nish is confused 'But, Thino, who was in the clump? Where did they come from? And why was it, Giselle?''.

The questions haunted Nish all through the history class, she thought, Giselle was not beautiful and according to her she was the most beautiful in the university; 'Though self-proclaimed'. She thought Giselle was conformable and naïve, totally incompatible with that mutinous and assertive Miach.

She sat in the history class near the window brooding as she couldn't find any scoop, she looked out of the window to see a tree divulge in front of her dispensing white flowers from it.

She shook her head to verify; thinking it was an illusion, but the next moment she looked back as she thought she had seen a shadow sitting amongst the branches of the tree. The tree had vanished, except for the glare of the sun that blinded her.

She thought about the vision and all of a sudden, she realized the tree is the one in the hostel garden. She thought 'Why is the tree shedding its flowers? …what significance? I am sure someone was amidst the branches, never mind' and she was back with her history books. At lunch break, she looked out the window and saw the same feature.

she summoned Thino "Thino, do you see the tree from our garden, there at the gate?" He replied, "No, there is nothing there, you have gone nuts".

Nish, "Maybe, I am seeing things"

Yeah right! He replied.

Thino pulled her and walked her to the cafeteria.

The tree continued projecting in her mind and it was shedding its flower and she was unable to get out of that illusion, questions were being raised in her mind.

 On the terrasse, at the cafeteria, there were two eyes were watching her, why…?

Chapter 11-Flustered and Revelation

That evening, the group gathered in Himu's room, all tensed and worried. They were all tired and the students of the university as well. Giselle had not come yet and it would be dinner time in another hour, they all awaited her for an answer to what had happened? After the previous night, they could not get together and discuss.

Quietude dominated the room; all were in their spree of thoughts with outrage in the back foot, as to why it happened. Abratos whimpered with pain and garrulously whined looking at his wound, about the previous night. He was extremely annoyed by the blustering and rampant murmured that he could not stop the scuffle and that boy in the hood did it. Abratos was carping," Those huge men were merciless, they could not stop thrashing this little thing I am". "This is all because of Giselle, I do not know what they think about her, she is so naïve and useless," he continued.

Miach yelled," Ohh! Stop it Abratos, let's understand the situation and find a solution".

Abratos continued, "I want to know; how did this spill out of the group, as those who came were not humans". "Let us ask Giselle when she comes".

Nish was in her chamber and the voice of some conversation could be heard faintly. Nish," Were you there when this happened? What did you see? Who was it?" She continued "I am so thrilled to hear".

A strong harsh voice responded, "Ohh! that was Aniktikus, you know him. He is always in haste, and sent out an alarm…, the alert is triggered. He never listens and took his so-called friends to create the scuffle. He has even-meddled with Giselle, I guess, and you know the consequence…". Instantly Nish intervened, "What is up with Giselle? What is she….", before she could complete, with a thud at the door, Thino barged in, "Who…? Who were you talking to?" he asked looking around to find someone there. Nish furious," You rat! how many times have I told you not to push into my room like that". Thino saw the creased bed cover on the unused bed and exclaimed, "Your secret, aah!

Nish asks him to shut up and go for dinner. Nish ponders',' Something is cooking'. They quickly move to the dining hall, where Nish sees Kanov quietly taking her dinner alone. Nish advances towards her table, "What happened today? that was a bad, very disobedient group with that Miach to lead, right! She arrogantly exclaims and turns with a jerk to move to her table.

Here in Miach's chamber all of them sit agitated, annoyed apprehending an explanation from Gisele. There is a knock at the door, Abratos yells, "Giselle, can you please come in". The door opens and Giselle steps in looking gorgeous and alluring as ever. Her laced pink gown flowing around her like a damsel transferred its glow onto her lovely face with a twinkle in her almond Mediterranean blue eyes appealing as ever.

Himu though angry could not resist his gaze into her deep blue eyes bedazzled and forgetting all the despise he had for her. Abratos, who was furious stood awestruck to see her with the slim delicate figure and the vibrance on her charming face on which one could instantly fall in love. Miach and Himu asked to come in and take a seat.

They sat quietly by the fireside, trying to recoup and reconcile with what had happened. Celosia and Kanov entered with a bowl of soup for everybody. They started consuming the soup, when Abratos recalled his pain and stood up, he looked at Giselle furious and asked, "Who was that fellow? How do you know him? and who was that hooded guy? seeing the silence and seemingly no response agitated him more.

Himu calmly, "Giselle, did you know this was coming? How could you be so insensitive? He continued, "And look at your atrocious behaviour, you keep mum and we do all the answering" "I do not know, why my dad is so supportive of you, I can't comprehend his visibility in you, I can't see anything".

Himu disdainfully grabs a chair to sit. Miach is dumbstruck at Himu's reaction as he was the calmest person. Giselle began to cry, Kanov went to console her, when Celosia began, "What is wrong with Kanov? Giselle is just a useless member of the group, she is the bugle blower for troubles, she got us bashed up" she continues "Kanov, you know, there was a guy in a hood, who was fighting for her, he vanished when we reached there".

Kanov," I was looking for you before you left, as I had sensed it and wanted to inform you of the danger, but could not find any of you" "Do you know, it was a plot to take Giselle away!" she exclaimed with a soft voice.

Ohh! Come on" said Abratos, "What is she; to be taken away, she is just a naïve nincompoop, who can't even stand for herself".

Himu retorts, "And they say she has come to save the world: from what? things are normal here ".

Quietness gripped the room except for the sobs of Giselle, her whimpering could be heard but made no difference to anyone except Miach and Damyan.

They went up to her and asked her to stop crying and not to heed them, as the others were raging with anger. Miach told her that this was the first time such a thing had happened. Miach also wanted to ask Giselle all the same questions about the incident and the hooded boy, it seemed to her that he was her acquaintance, but her sob refrained Miach. Damyan also felt sorry for Giselle and there was very little he could do about it.

At the gate, Mr Warbhinger was awoken by the odour and the noise, he looked up and around, stifled barged into his watcher cabin.

The clouds in the area were getting thicker and darker, the murmuring of the starlings also shaped in the sky with the loud whistling and trilling of the birds escalating. A timelapse aura with a tinge of blue and green was seen building up in the sky. The stephanotis was vibrating and swaying releasing a strange odour with a light blue colour fume, which permeated the air adding to the aura.

The sound of waves at sea could be heard screaming and roaring, as though they were lashing against each other in competition. The displays at the dining hall flashed all of a sudden and Sir Megnanissus appeared to be speaking on the screen, the hostel keeper Madame Nagasevani, ran towards the screen as she had no intimation of any announcement; but the screen was wildly pixelating, flickering off and on and in a while went silent. The next moment the watcher was seen entering with a smoking thurible, he passed through the maze of tables children seated slowly began tilting onto the table, while their dishes manoeuvred to make way for their resting heads.

When Madame Nagasevani sees Warbhinger's action she asked, " What has happened?

He replied, "Know not, just following orders".

In the chamber, Giselle continued to sob, when Himu again got up from his seat," Why are you quiet, don't show us your tears, tell us" Continued Abratos vehemently, "Giselle, please tell us why are you here? Giselle shook with fear at this uproar and started crying.

In the next movement, Himu took a vase kept beside the bed and smashed it on the ground out of rage, Damyan tried consoling him., Just then Kanov started releasing the colours of Blue and red, she said," wait" and waved her hand to stop, the next instant there was thumping at the door and the door opened, Warbhinger and Madame Nagasevani, barged in and in chorus, "What's happening…?

The boys instead retorted back, "Who is this, Giselle? …"

Just then the sounds of the ocean; with the trilling and whistling overwhelmed the room, a foul oceanic smell enveloped the room.

Before anything could be realised, a strong majestic figure appeared, glistening probably with water surfaced all over him, followed by the three nymphs. Next Sir Prakinasus and Sir Megnanissus popped in from the open window. All present in the room were taken by surprise, while Giselle was unaware of what was happening.

The personable radiant figure; a staggering stalwart with stunning tall stature was wearing an ancient Greek outfit and looked like a lion from his den. There was a dazzling belt running over his chest and had glowing starfish stuck over it, a crown of gold studded with gems with a fish structure on it burdened his head.

As he appeared, he stumped his sceptre with golden and silver carvings and had some gems here and there on it. A huge blue octopus rested on its orb with its tentacles circulating the staff and over the king. The orb and large aquamarine could be visible off and on as the octopus moved.

The majestic figure declared, "I, king Puissant from the Shinisus dynasty, Son of Majodar Shinisus Protector of the realm-the world, Ruler of the Oceans, The Land and the Space, The Mightiest of the mighty, I with my two mighty men, guard the world against kakó daímona (evil demons) and the dark riders, the suffering inflictor, the gobbler of souls and the owner of the winged horse".

All of them bow their heads to the mighty, Giselle lifts her head and runs to hug the king.

King puissant continues, "I have been anointed by the Divine Father Dias against callous Pysipus-the destructor, exiled to Kur, he is designing his return accompanied by destruction and pain. You are all my army…".

He pauses for a moment and continues in a terrifying bawl, "Hail! Regina Puella Giselle, The Fortis! This is my only daughter Giselle, the mighty from the Shinisus dynasty, the brave, heir to the mighty kingdom of Miiletus, successor to my throne, future protector of the realm-the world, the ocean and the galaxy".

He pauses and then continues, "Her might stretches from the powerful watchtowers to the power of the minds, the oceans, the space and beyond. She is the controls nature and the venom of the stephanotis. She is the commander of the commandments of the Alpha and has been appointed for days ahead to protect the strike on the human world" He continues, "The wrath has been unleashed, Giselle is your princess and is here to guide and support you".

Prakinasus also addresses," We were closing watching you, my generals did not fall true to our anticipation despite the warnings sent. There is suffering, pain, diseases, fire devised by the evil and war that could take lives, and we are their only help".

He glorifies the king and the princess and proclaims, "All Bow"

"Hail our princess! Hail Giselle! Hail King Puissant!"

The king gently lets his daughter by the hand and Giselle rise with all glory as instructed by her father; all bowed in front of her.

Giselle manifested her true magnificent self and rose high, all present looked at her fortis and found a true leader. The faces in the chamber are all shown with confidence as they looked on at the vibrance and spillage of power. Her radiance was no bound as she showed the virtue of the colours around her; split into a tree, fluttering butterflies and a whole lot of flowers that showered on them, she imbued yellow and gold into the air giving joy and hope with the sweet fragrant aroma that suffused happiness. There was a consolidation of assurance and determination that loaded the minds of Himu and Miach. She gradually and elegantly reinstated to herself after a splendorous appearance. Seeing Giselle the members of the group thought how insensitive could they be.

Giselle spoke," My father sent me here to help with the unprecedented, for the cause of the living we protect. We are the strong militia of Corinth; let us work together. I was quiet and subdued because of my protocols and as my father wanted. we need to keep in mind our skills are groomed with the sharpener of discipline and obedience, and my father had to come for me, who knew, I would bear but not budge'. She looks at her father, who thumps again with his sceptre, with the surging roar of waves and the whistling they all disappear.

Himu, Miach, Kanov and Giselle team up with the others and await the unprecedented. Abratos feels dejected and awkward for all that he had said to Giselle but she consoles him, while the others approach her with acceptance. Nish continues to be sedated in the dining hall as she was taken off guard.

Giselle looks outside the window and realises; the cooling has been done for the moment. She thinks,' The worst is yet…'. Standing near the window, she looks out to a distance, where the watchtowers seem to bow to her and a blue light seems to travel far and gradually diminish to fade away. Slowly, she turns her back to the window and smiles…